Sports Stars

ISIAH THOMAS

Pocket Magic

By Bert Rosenthal

CHILDRENS PRESS ™

CHICAGO

Cover photograph: Ira N. Golden
Inside photographs courtesy of the following:
Allen M. Einstein, pages 6, 11, 16, 20, 22, 24, 26, 28, 31, 33, 39, 41, and 43
Carl V. Sissac, pages 9 and 37
Peter Travers, pages 14 and 35
Ira N. Golden, page 18

Library of Congress Cataloging in Publishing Data

Rosenthal, Bert.
   Isiah Thomas, Pocket Magic.

   (Sport stars)
   Summary: A biography of the basketball player from
Chicago who plays for the Detroit Pistons during the
basketball season and during the summer attends Indiana
University, where he is studying to be a lawyer.
   1. Thomas, Isiah, 1961-   —Juvenile literature.
2. Basketball players—United States—Biography—Juvenile
literature. [1. Thomas, Isiah, 1961-   . 2. Basketball players.
3. Afro-Americans—Biography]
I. Title. II. Series.
GV884.T47R67 1983   796.32'3'0924 [B] [92] 83-10080
ISBN 0-516-04334-X

   3 4 5 6 7 8 9 10 11 12 R 90 89 88 87 86 85

Sports Stars

ISIAH THOMAS

Pocket Magic

Isiah Thomas is a winner.

He is a winning basketball player.

He is a winner with his family, especially with his mother.

He is a winner with young children.

He is a winner in the classroom.

He is a winner with friends.

He is a winner with his teammates.

And he has a winning smile.

Isiah is a professional basketball player. He plays for the Detroit Pistons. The Pistons are a team in the National Basketball Association.

The Pistons never have won the league title. But Isiah is helping them win many games. He scores a lot of points. He also helps other players score points. He looks for a player in a good position. Then he passes the ball to them. When they are in good position, they can score, too.

Isiah enjoys making a good pass as much as he enjoys scoring. If another player on his team scores, it counts just as much as if Isiah scored.

What matters most to Isiah is that the Pistons win.

"I just want to win as many games as possible," he said. "That's the only goal I have."

Isiah loves playing basketball. Even though it is a job, he doesn't look upon it as a job.

"It's my hobby," he said. "I'm happy doing it. Most people don't get paid for doing something they like."

Isiah gets paid a lot of money for doing what he likes. His pay is about $400,000 a year.

He gives a lot of his money to his family. Especially to his mother, Mary Thomas.

Isiah's mother raised Isiah and his eight brothers and sisters. Isiah was the youngest of the children. He was born April 30, 1961. His father left home when Isiah was three years old.

Isiah is the youngest of the nine Thomas children. Many of his brothers and sisters now have children of their own. Here we see most of Isiah's family. His mother is in the last row, second in from the right.

So, Isiah's mother had to bring up the children.

It wasn't easy. Not with nine children. So, when Isiah grew up he was thankful for all his mother had done. And when he got a lot of money, he bought his mother a house near Chicago.

Isiah and his brothers and sisters had lived in Chicago when they were young. They lived in a bad part of the city. So, when Isiah could, he took his mother out of the bad area.

"I talk to my mom a lot," he said. "She's doing okay. And I miss her, too. I miss all of my family."

Isiah doesn't get to see his family as much as he would like. He spends a lot of time playing basketball. Isiah has to go to training camp with the Pistons in September. The season begins in October. It doesn't end until April.

It could end even later if the Pistons are really good. Then they would go into the playoffs. And if the Pistons make it to the final playoff series, they would play until June. That's a long season.

After the season Isiah works in his camp. It's called the Isiah Thomas Basketball Camp of Champions. It's in the Detroit area. It's for boys and girls 8 to 18 years old.

Isiah enjoys teaching basketball to kids.

"I've worked a lot of camps where kids spend their money and don't learn anything," he said. "They go there and just fool around a lot. I just teach the kids the simple things about basketball."

Isiah finds the job of teaching satisfying.

"There are a lot of people who teach basketball, but they don't know the game," he said. "They read books on it. They think they can teach it. I'm ready to teach it. I like it. I like to teach youngsters because they are willing to learn. I say something, they listen."

After the basketball season Isiah also goes to Indiana University. That's where he started college. He went to college for only two years.

It doesn't matter if the young basketball players are girls or boys, Isiah wants to help them all.

Then he left to play professional basketball. But Isiah wants to get his college degree. That's why he goes to school during the summer. He is studying to be a lawyer when he finishes playing basketball.

Isiah needs to take more courses before he can get his degree. Without his degree, he cannot become a lawyer.

"My mother made me sign a contract that I would go and get my degree," Isiah said.

Isiah said he wants to be a lawyer so he can help people stay out of jail.

"When I grew up on the West Side of Chicago, a lot of people were committing crimes," he said, "like stealing a pair of pants. Or a shirt. And they are doing 10 years in jail.

"It's sad that those guys didn't have some-body to speak for them," said Isiah. "They couldn't afford a lawyer. I'd like to go back there and help."

Isiah said he has thought about helping those people for several years.

"I said when I was in a position where I could help, I was going to try to help them," he said.

Isiah also tries to help youngsters at his camp. Basketball is not the only thing he teaches them. He also tells them about the importance of going to school.

"Getting an education is important," he said.

A good education will help keep youngsters out of trouble. That's why Isiah tells them to go to school.

A good education also will help them get a better job. That, too, is important.

By working for his college degree now, Isiah is planning for the future. He knows he can't play basketball forever. When his playing days are over, that's when he hopes to become a lawyer.

Another thing Isiah does during the summer is get together with Magic Johnson. Magic is one of his best friends. Magic also plays pro basketball. He is with the Los Angeles Lakers.

Isiah poses with his friend Magic and Dr. Charles Tucker,
a business associate.

Magic is very tall. He is 6-foot-8. Isiah is only 6-foot-1. That's why some people call him "Pocket Magic."

Magic and Pocket Magic have a lot in common. First, of course, they like to play basketball. Both are exciting players.

Magic calls Isiah "Mr. Excitement."

"You want to come see some hoop-de-doop, you come see Isiah," said Magic.

"We're together every day in the summer," Johnson said. "You can't separate us. If we can't get together during the week, we get together on weekends. We have the same interests. We just get along."

Kent Benson, Isiah, Kelly Tripucka, and the general manager of the Pistons, Jack McCloskey, at the 1982 awards presentation.

Both like to smile a lot. It's a big part of their personality. They smile because they enjoy life. They're happy with what they're doing. And they like to show it.

A lot of people compare Isiah with Magic. They do it because of their smiles and their friendliness. What does Isiah think about being compared with Magic?

"I love it," he said. "There aren't any other Magic Johnsons around. It's a compliment."

Both Pocket Magic and Magic began playing basketball when they were very young.

Isiah poses for a picture with one of his young fans. After the basketball season, Isiah teaches youngsters how to play basketball.

Isiah started playing when he was only three years old. At that age, he could dribble the ball and shoot it. He was really amazing. He was so good that he used to put on a show during the halftime of games played by older boys.

When Isiah was in kindergarten he was as good as some of the older boys. His first coach has a picture of him shooting a lay-up when he was in kindergarten.

"I was really a peewee then," said Isiah.

By the time Isiah was in fourth grade he was playing on a team with eighth graders. And he was the team leader!

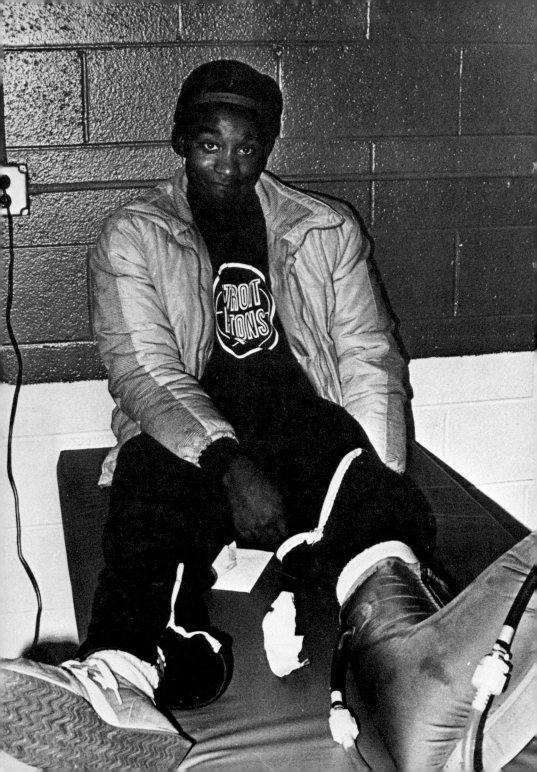

It was his job to handle the ball. It was an important job. But Isiah did it well. It didn't matter that the boys he played against were much older. He could play as well as they.

After Isiah finished the eighth grade, he wanted to go to a certain high school. The school had a very good basketball team. But the coach didn't want him. The coach told Isiah he was too small. Isiah was only 5-foot-6. One of his brothers told the coach that Isiah would grow much taller. But the coach didn't listen. Isiah was disappointed.

He wound up going to another high school.

That school was a long way from home. It was a mile and a half away. Isiah had to take the train and a bus to get there.

He got up at 5:30 in the morning.

Sometimes, when he was leaving, it was dark. And his mother would start to cry. She wanted life to be easier for Isiah. But she was too poor to make it better.

Isiah knew it was not easy on her. That's why he wanted to make it easier for her when he grew up.

"There's not anything I could do or say that could repay my mother," he said. "Not for all the years she gave me and my family. My mother worked hard all her life. She didn't earn much

money. After my father left, my mom kept us together by herself. She worked at a lot of jobs. She did whatever she could."

In Isiah's first year in high school, he played a lot of basketball. But he didn't study much. He nearly flunked out of school.

The school basketball coach told Isiah that it was important to study. He told him he needed good grades to get a scholarship to college. Isiah listened. He listened well.

He studied hard. And each of the next three years he made the school's honor roll.

He also led the basketball team to second place in the state high school tournament. And he was named a high school All-America.

Because he was a good basketball player and a good student, he got a lot of offers to go to college. He chose Indiana University because it was close to home. He went to Indiana on a basketball scholarship.

Isiah's mother liked the Indiana coach, Bobby Knight. The coach told Mrs. Thomas that Isiah would get a good education. He also told her Isiah would get a good chance to be a better basketball player.

He got both.

He became known for his basketball playing.

In his first year at Indiana, Isiah was chosen to play for the United States team in the Pan

American Games. The United States basketball team won the gold medal—first place—at the Games. In the final game Isiah played very well. He scored 21 points. He had five steals, and he had four assists.

That year Isiah also helped Indiana University win its league title. And he was named to the All-League Team.

Before the start of his second year at Indiana, Isiah was chosen to another United States team. This was the 1980 Olympic team. But the United States chose not to compete in the Olympics. So, Isiah lost his chance for another gold medal.

However, the team did go on a tour of the United States. And Isiah helped the team win four of five games they played.

On that tour Isiah played against his friend Magic. That was the first time they had played against each other. Late in the game, Thomas fouled out. On his way to the bench, Magic shook his hand. And Magic told him that he was a very good player.

"It really made me feel good, coming from him," said Isiah. "Because he's such a great person. And then he smiled. I couldn't help but smile back."

That was the start of their friendship.

After that, Isiah began his second year at Indiana.

During the season Isiah and Magic sometimes play against one another.
In the summer they can play on the same team.

The team was better. And so was Isiah. The team won the national title.

In the final game, Isiah scored 23 points. He had five assists, and he had four steals.

He also was named the outstanding player in the championship tournament.

When the game ended a lot of Indiana University fans rushed onto the court. One was Isiah's mother.

Isiah met her near the center of the court. They hugged each other. She was crying. And Isiah appeared close to tears.

"Thanks, Mom," Isiah said. "Thanks for everything you've gone through for me. I hope I can do something for you."

Isiah's mother talks to ABC news in Detroit.

A short time later Isiah got his chance to do something for his mother.

It happened when the Pistons chose him in the NBA draft. He was picked on the first round. He was the second player chosen.

The first player chosen was another youngster who had grown up in Chicago. He was Mark Aguirre of DePaul University. He was taken by the Dallas team.

The Pistons paid a lot of money to sign his contract. Isiah signed to play for the team for four years.

He played very well his first year. In his first game as a pro he scored 31 points. He also had 11 assists.

Isiah is always willing to sign autographs. He has just signed a fan's painting of Indiana University at the NCAA.

He finished the season with a 17-point average.

His second season was even better. That year he scored about 20 points a game.

There is little doubt that Isiah has a bright future. Both as a basketball player and as a lawyer. Isiah Thomas is a winner. No matter what he does.

CHRONOLOGY

1961—Isiah Thomas is born April 30.

1964—Isiah begins playing basketball at the age of three.

1975—He enrolls in St. Joseph's High School in Westchester, Illinois.

1979—Isiah leads St. Joseph's to second place in the Illinois state high school tournament. He is chosen a high school All-America.

1979—Isiah is chosen to the United States basketball team for the Pan American Games. The team wins the gold medal, as Isiah scores 21 points in the title game.

1979—Isiah enrolls in Indiana University on a basketball scholarship.

1980—Indiana wins the Big Ten Conference title and Isiah is named to the All-League Team as a freshman.

1980—He is picked for the United States Olympic Basketball team.

1981—Indiana again wins the Big Ten title and Isiah again is chosen to the All-League Team. Indiana also wins the NCAA title and Isiah is named the championship tournament's outstanding player.

1981—Isiah is chosen on the first round of the National Basketball Association draft by the Detroit Pistons. He signs a four-year contract with the Pistons for a total of $1.6 million.

1982—Isiah is named a starter for the East team in the NBA All-Star Game.

1982—In his first season in the NBA, Isiah averages 17 points a game and is selected to the All-Rookie Team.

1983—Isiah again is chosen as a starter for the East team in the NBA All-Star Game.

1984—Isiah signs a "lifetime" contract with the Pistons after a successful season. His playing helps (21 points, 15 assists, 5 rebounds, and 4 steals) the East beat the West in the highest scoring All-Star game in NBA history. Isiah is awarded the MVP trophy.

1985—Although the East loses in the NBA All-Star game, Isiah is the high scorer with 22 points.

ABOUT THE AUTHOR

Bert Rosenthal has worked for the Associated Press for nearly 25 years. He has covered or written about virtually every sport. Mr. Rosenthal is the author of Sports Stars books on Larry Bird, Marques Johnson, Sugar Ray Leonard, Darryl Dawkins, and Wayne Gretzky.

He was AP's pro basketball editor from 1973 until 1976. From 1974 until early 1980, he was the secretary-treasurer of the Professional Basketball Writers' Association of America. He has been a co-author on two books—*Pro Basketball Superstars of 1974* and *Pro Basketball Superstars of 1975*. For the past five years Mr. Rosenthal has been editor of HOOP Magazine, an official publication of the National Basketball Association.

At present, he is the AP's track and field editor, and a frequent contributor to many basketball, football, and baseball magazines.